WITHDRAWN FROM
COLLECTION

Sneezy the Snowman

by
Maureen Wright

illustrated by
Stephen Gilpin

Marshall Cavendish Children

Text copyright © 2010 by Maureen Wright
Illustrations copyright © 2010 by Stephen Gilpin
All rights reserved

Marshall Cavendish Corporation, 99 White Plains Road, Tarrytown, NY 10591
www.marshallcavendish.us/kids

Library of Congress Cataloging-in-Publication Data

Wright, Maureen, 1961-
Sneezy the snowman / Maureen Wright ; [illustrations by] Stephen Gilpin.
—1st ed.
p. cm.
Summary: A snowman who finds it dreadfully cold keeps doing things that
cause him to melt, while the children who rebuild him each time offer
clothing to keep him warm.
ISBN 978-0-7614-5711-4
[1. Stories in rhyme. 2. Snowmen—Fiction. 3. Clothing and dress—Fiction.
4. Humorous stories.] I. Gilpin, Stephen, ill. II. Title.
PZ8.3.W93635ne 2010
2009043646

The illustrations were drawn by hand and colored in Photoshop.
Book design by Anahid Hamparian
Editor: Margery Cuyler

Printed in Malaysia (T)
First edition

1 3 5 6 4 2

mc Marshall Cavendish
Children

With gratitude to my editor, Margery Cuyler
—M.W.

For Angie
—S.G.

Sneezy the Snowman shivered, "Br-r-r.
It's cold out here, that's for sure.
I need a drink to warm me up!"
So . . .

he drank cocoa from a cup.
He said with a smile, "I like this a lot."

And then—right there—believe it or not . . .

he melted from drinking something too hot!
The children cried out, "What should we do?"
A voice from the puddle said, "Make me brand new."

MORTON MANDAN PUBLIC LIBRARY

They rebuilt Sneezy as snowflakes flew.
A cold winter wind swirled and blew.

The snowman sneezed a gigantic ACHOO!
"I'm sneezing and freezing and shivering too!"
A little girl said, "Then let's share,
I have something you can wear.
Here's my hat to put on your head."

"You look awesome!" the children said.
The snowman blinked his coal-black eyes—
the stocking cap was a nice surprise.

But Sneezy the Snowman shivered, "Br-r-r.
It's cold out here, that's for sure.
I am freezing every minute.
I'll find a hot tub and sit right in it."

He found one and smiled. "I like this a lot."

And then—right there—believe it or not . . .

he melted from sitting in water too hot!
The children cried out, "What should we do?"
A voice from the hot tub said,

They rebuilt Sneezy as snowflakes flew.
A cold winter wind swirled and blew.

The snowman sneezed a gigantic ACHOO!

"I'm sneezing and freezing and shivering too!"

A little boy said, "Then let's share.

I have something you can wear.

Here's my scarf that's red and blue.

I think it would look great on you."

The snowman blinked his coal-black eyes.
The colorful scarf was a nice surprise.

It went very well with the long pink hat.
The children all said, "How about that!"

But Sneezy the Snowman shivered, "Br-r-r.
It's cold out here, that's for sure.

I need to feel some warmth on me.
There's a campfire by that tree."

He said with a smile, "I like this a lot."
And then—right there—believe it or not . . .
he melted from standing beside something hot!
The children cried out, "What should we do?"
A voice from the puddle said,

MAKE ME BRAND NEW!

They rebuilt Sneezy as snowflakes flew.
A cold winter wind swirled and blew.

The snowman sneezed a gigantic ACHOO!
"I'm sneezing and freezing and shivering too!"
A little girl said, "Then let's share.
I have something you can wear.
Here's my coat—the perfect fit.
I know that you'll look good in it."

The snowman blinked his coal-black eyes.
The bright-orange coat was a nice surprise.
It went very well with the scarf and hat.
The children all said, "How about that!"

But Sneezy said, "Whew, I'm way too hot!
I'll take off all the new clothes I've got."

The children yelled, "No! That's not the way.
Listen to what we have to say—
buy something cold at the ice cream store.
Have two scoops—or three—or four!"

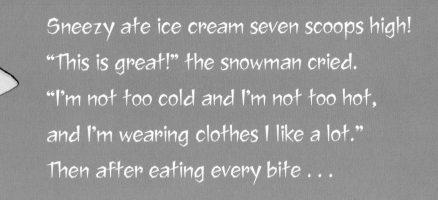

Sneezy ate ice cream seven scoops high!
"This is great!" the snowman cried.
"I'm not too cold and I'm not too hot,
and I'm wearing clothes I like a lot."
Then after eating every bite . . .

he said, "At last! I feel just right."